Clifford TAKES A TRIP

Clifford
TAKES A TRIP

Story and pictures by NORMAN BRIDWELL

SCHOLASTIC BOOK SERVICES

NEW YORK • LONDON • RICHMOND HILL, ONTARIO

To Tracy

1st printing...September 1966

Printed in the U.S.A.

Hi, I'm Emily Elizabeth.
This is a happy day for me.

This is the last day of school.
Summer vacation is here!
Now I can play with my dog Clifford.

We don't go on long vacation trips.
It's too hard to get Clifford on a bus
or train.

We only go to places that Clifford can walk to, like picnics in the park.

Last year was different.
Last year we went to the mountains.
Mommy and Daddy said it was too far
for Clifford to walk.

So we left him with the lady next door.

That night Clifford was so lonely . . .

. . . he began to howl. He howled
and he howled and he howled —

— until someone threw a shoe at him.
It didn't hurt Clifford's nose,
but it did hurt his feelings.

The next morning Clifford set out to find us.
He sniffed his way along the road.

Clifford didn't mean to make trouble.
But a lot of people had never seen
a big red dog before.

Clifford kept going.
Nothing could stop him.

And then he saw a little old man
trying to fix his truck.
The man needed help.

So Clifford stopped and helped him.
He took the little old man to a garage.

The little old man gave Clifford a little lunch,
to thank him for his help.

Then Clifford set out again.
Nothing stopped him — not even wet cement.

And traffic jams didn't stop him.
Clifford just tip-toed over the cars.
And then . . .

. . . he came to a toll bridge.
Clifford had no money.

But that didn't stop him.

We didn't know Clifford was coming.

I found some new playmates —
two baby bears.

I was having so much fun.
And then Mama Bear came.

Mama Bear didn't want strangers to play with her babies. She growled.

Then we heard a LOUDER growl.
Guess who was growling!

Mama Bear was surprised.

She even forgot her babies.
I told Clifford that the Mama Bear
was only protecting her children.

Good old Clifford took the baby bears
back to Mama Bear.

Then he took us all back to camp.
Mommy and Daddy were surprised
to see Clifford.

I told them how Clifford saved my life.

So they let Clifford stay with us.

Next year, maybe we will find a way
to take Clifford with us
when we go on vacation.